Three Is Company

Weekly Reader Children's Book Club presents

Three Is Company

by
Friedrich Karl Waechter

translated by
Harry Allard

Doubleday & Company, Inc. Garden City, New York

Library of Congress Cataloging in Publication Data

Waechter, Friedrich Karl.
  Three is company.

  Translation of Wir können noch viel zusammen
machen.
  SUMMARY: A pig, a bird, and a fish make friends,
although their parents think it is strange.
  [1. Friendship—Fiction. 2. Animals—Fiction]
I. Allard, Harry. II. Title.
PZ7.W1198Th 1980   [E]

Library of Congress Catalog Card Number 79-7790
ISBN: 0-385-14632-9 Trade. 0-385-14633-7 Prebound

Three Is Company

 "Being the only little fish in the fishpond isn't exactly fun, you know."

"Mommy and Daddy are here, Harold."

 "But if I had a playmate my own age, I'd have a lot more fun."

"Well, there just aren't any little fish your own age in the
fishpond, Harold. But you can still have fun."
 "Phooey!"
"But, Harold, it's true." 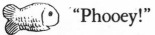 "What kind of fun?"

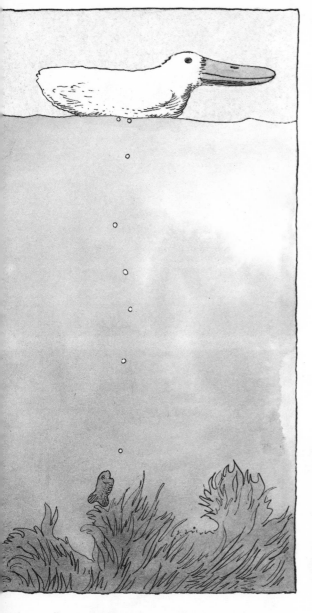

"Well, let's see.... You can always tickle the duck with
bubbles...."
 "Yes, but if I had playmates, it would be twice as
much fun."

"And you've always loved tangling up the fishermen's lines."

"Yes, but if I had a playmate, it would be even more fun."

"Now, Harold, don't you just love leaping in and out of the water?"

"Yes, but if I had playmates, it would be *ten* times as much fun."

"Be patient, Harold. After all, a little brother or sister is not entirely out of the question."

 "When?"

"Oh, in a year or so."

 "By then I'll be too old for kid stuff."

"Never satisfied, are you, Harold?"

 "Being the only little pig in the barnyard isn't exactly fun, you know."

"Now, Ivy, stop complaining."  "Hmmm..."

"Just exactly what do you mean by 'Hmmm,' Ivy?"

 "If I had a playmate my own age, I'd have a lot more fun."

"Now, Ivy, don't you just love cutting up with old Cleo out in the cow pasture?" "Hmmm..."

"And pestering crabby old Uncle Clarence in the poultry yard?"   "Hmmm..."

"And rolling in the lovely mud in the swamp?"

"Hmmm..."

"And don't you just love trotting behind Daddy?"

"And taking a Sunday stroll through the fields and meadows with Mommy and Daddy?"

   "I'd rather have someone my own age to play with."

"Never satisfied, are you, Ivy?"

"Being the only little bird in the treetops isn't exactly fun, you know."

"Philip, why are you complaining? You have a lovely life up here."

"Mommy is forever piloting you wherever you want to go..."

"And Daddy often swings you..."

"And takes you sight-seeing . . ."

"And coaches your flying practice."

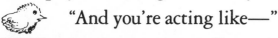 "But I'm bored. I want to do something I've never done before."

"Why don't you practice your loop-the-looping? Or make believe you're a butterfly?"

"Phooey! I want to roll in the mud like a pig or swim in the pond like a fish."

"Philip, you're acting like a baby!"

"And you're acting like—"

"Philip, watch your tongue!"

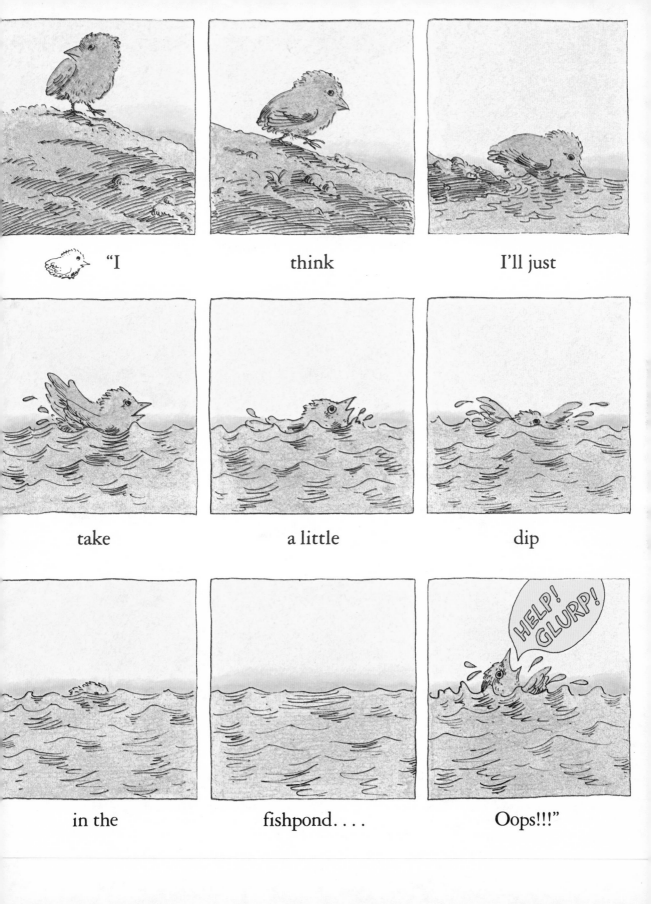

"I   think   I'll just

take   a little   dip

in the   fishpond. . . .   Oops!!!"

 "Hello. May I ask what you're doing?"

"I'm trying to learn to swim. But I just can't get the hang of it."

 "May I show you?" "Yes, would you?"

 "Why don't you practice near the shore first? By the way, my name is Harold."

 "And mine's Philip."

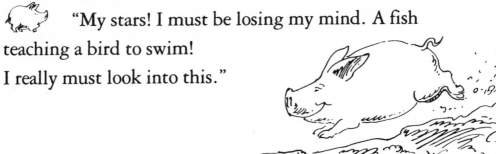 "My stars! I must be losing my mind. A fish teaching a bird to swim! I really must look into this."

 "Hi. I'm Ivy. May I play, too?" "Yes. Welcome to the Beginners' Swimming Class."

"Why, Ivy, you swim like an angel." "Thank you." "But I bet you can't fly, Ivy."

 "No, I can't." "Can you fly, Harold?" "Just a tiny bit. About a foot out of the water, that's all."

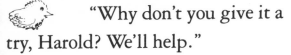 "But I'm no good at all at walking or running."

"Why don't you give it a try, Harold? We'll help."

"You're doing beautifully, Harold." "Would you two teach me to swim?"

"Sure."

"Would you two teach me to fly?"

"To tell the truth, Ivy, I really don't think we could manage *that*."

"Well, what else could we do together?"

 "Let's see. . . . What about rubbing noses together?"

"And what else?"

 "We could bump bottoms together."

"And we could always touch tummies together."

"You know, I think there's really no end to the things that we can do together."

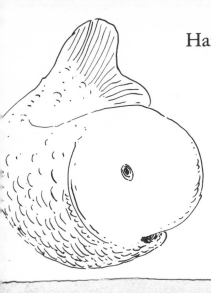

Harold's parents were puzzled:
"Harold has been
on the go constantly.
I wonder if it
could have anything
to do with his
two funny friends?"

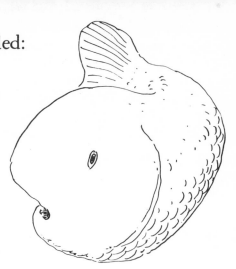

Ivy's parents did not know
what to make of it:
"Ivy has been
so nice lately.
Could it have
anything to do with
her two strange friends?"

Philip's parents could not get over it:
"Philip is much more cheerful
these days. Do you think it
has something to do with
his two unusual
friends?"

FRIEDRICH KARL WAECHTER, born in Danzig, Germany, in 1937, grew up in Schleswig-Holstein and later attended the Alsterdamm Art School in Hamburg. After working in advertising and publishing for several years, Mr. Waechter began to free-lance for various publishers, and he has concentrated on his own writing and illustrating since 1966. Among his published works are a play version of *The Bremen Town Musicians*, a book called *The Anti-Struwwelpeter*, and THREE IS COMPANY.

HARRY ALLARD, who translated THREE IS COMPANY from the German, is a professor of foreign languages at Salem State College in Massachusetts and holds degrees from Northwestern and Yale University. Among his many books for children are *It's So Nice to Have a Wolf Around the House* and *Bumps in the Night*. Mr. Allard makes his home in Charlestown, Massachusetts.